PILOT SEASON

PILOT SEASON

James Brubaker

SUNNYOUTSIDE
Buffalo

Acknowledgments

The author would like to thank Shannon Hozinec at Vector Press and Bayard Godsave at *The Oklahoma Review* for publishing excerpts from *Pilot Season* in their earlier forms.

ISBN: 978-1-934513-46-0
Library of Congress Control Number: 2014932173

sunnyoutside
PO Box 911
Buffalo, NY 14207
USA

www.sunnyoutside.com

Pilots

Pilot Season 1

In this hour-long drama, a beleaguered television network executive fights to keep his job and earn the respect of his family. The Executive is in charge of programming and project development at a fictional television network. Unfortunately for The Executive, The Network's ratings have been in decline for three years, and the series begins with The Network's CEO informing The Executive that if The Network's fortunes aren't reversed in the upcoming television season, the entire programming and project development department will be replaced with younger, hipper executives. With this new imperative from The CEO, The Executive sets out to find a slate of television shows that might attract an audience, and save The Network from its embarrassing decline. Additionally, as The Executive has spent the previous three years working hard only to produce subpar programming, his family views him as failure. This would be more of a problem than it might be, but The Executive rarely spends time with his family. As such, *Pilot Season* finds The Executive attempting to reconnect with his family and earn their respect at the same time that he is trying to save his network and his job. In the pilot episode, after the dire meeting with The CEO, The Executive calls his wife to say hello. She is not particularly interested in talking to him, so she puts The Son on the phone. When The Executive asks The Son about his day, The Son says, "It was fine." When The Executive asks The Son about school and baseball practice, The Son tells his father they are both "fine." Clearly growing bored with the conversation, The Son hands the phone to The Daughter, and a similar conversation ensues. After the phone conversation, The

Executive eats fast-food tacos alone in his office and sends emails to creative teams about developing pilots. The Executive arranges to meet with a number of creative teams about commissioning new shows. As the pilot episode ends, The Executive arrives at a creative meeting for a new show set to be called...

A Father's Love 2

This elimination-style, reality television show finds several contestants competing for the love of a father. This is neither the actual father of any of the contestants, nor an almighty Father—it is simply a man who happens to be a father. The contestants compete in challenges such as making breakfast for The Father, buying Father's Day gifts for The Father, playing sports with The Father, working on car engines with The Father, bathing The Father, bringing The Father his pornographic magazines when he is in the bathroom, reading the newspaper to The Father, massaging The Father's feet, bringing home an appropriate significant other who pleases The Father, agreeing with The Father's political beliefs, appreciating the significance of The Father's generation's contributions to society, making things out of wood for and with The Father, not telling anyone when you see The Father ogle waitresses, cleaning The Father's collection of Civil War memorabilia, painting a cubist portrait of The Father, siding with The Father when he talks about all the times his wife cheated on him, carving dice out of bone for The Father, and helping The Father inside and to bed when he comes home drunk and throws up on the porch. At the conclusion of each episode, The Father selects one contestant and dismisses him or her by saying, "I'm very disappointed in you." In the pilot episode, the contestants are invited to a formal dinner where they meet The Father for the first time. There is no formal contest in this first episode, but The Father decides to dismiss a male contestant who refrains from ordering an alcoholic beverage despite The Father's insistence. After the young man leaves the dinner table, The Father says, "Never trust a man who won't drink with you. Men like that, they will always find ways to make you feel bad about yourselves." The show's finale features the last three contestants eulogizing The Father at a mock funeral, after which The Father selects the son or daughter he loves most as the winner.

Buddies 3

A sitcom about two friends, The Fat One and The Pretty One, who share an efficiency apartment. The Pretty One and his friends delight in finding new ways to say mean, but funny, things to The Fat One, several times an episode. The Fat One always accidentally interferes when The Pretty One is trying to have sex. In the pilot episode, The Pretty One is about to have sex with a woman when The Fat One returns home from his job at a call center, intending to eat hamburgers out of a grease-soaked sack and watch episodes of popular science fiction television shows. The Fat One's presence in such a small apartment prevents The Pretty One and his lady friend from having sex. Also, the Pretty One's lady friend wants to leave because she is disgusted by The Fat One and his sack of hamburgers. In his frustration, The Pretty One throws The Fat One's sack of hamburgers out the window. When The Fat One runs out of the apartment to retrieve his sack of hamburgers, The Pretty One locks and chains the door behind him, apologizes to his lady friend, and then the two have sex. The pilot episode ends on a happy note because The Fat One retrieves his sack of hamburgers before any of the neighborhood dogs or homeless people steal it. With his sack of hamburgers tucked under his arm, The Fat One tries to get back into the efficiency apartment that he shares with The Pretty One, but can't because the door is chained. When he tries to open the door, he can hear The Pretty One and his lady friend having sex. The Fat One sits down in the hallway outside of his apartment and eats his hamburgers and is happy. The Audience laughs and feels uplifted by The Fat One's positive attitude in the face of being so fat and disrespected. In the episode's final scene, which plays behind the closing credits, we see that The Fat One is asleep in the hallway, hugging the now empty sack of hamburgers. The Pretty One and his lady friend, with whom he was having sex, open the door of the efficiency apartment and cover The Fat One with a blanket. The Audience says, "Awwwww," then The Pretty One and the woman go back inside and have more sex.

Outside the Box 4

This reality-style, elimination-based game show brings together a group of young misfits to socialize, drink, and squeeze themselves into boxes. *Outside the Box* is a weekly contest designed to test contestants' flexibility. The focus of each episode is a "Box Challenge" in which contestants attempt to fit themselves into various containers that shrink and change shape every week. The "Box Challenge" runs throughout each episode, intercut with footage from the week leading up to the challenge, which shows the contestants training and fraternizing with each other. At the conclusion of each episode, the contestants vote one of their peers *Outside the Box*. The only contestants safe from each week's elimination are those who fit themselves into their boxes during the challenge. In the pilot episode, The Audience will learn that one of the contestants is a contortionist—a plant introduced by the producers to provide added tension and drama. Over the course of the season, the contestants—including the young one, the sexy one, the homosexual one, the belligerent one, the old one, and the one who is a mother—will try to squeeze themselves into a diverse array of containers such as the trunk of a small car, an industrial-sized oven, a tuba case, a tuba, and a series of drain pipes from beneath a kitchen sink, among others. The first week's "Box Challenge" tasks the competitors with positioning themselves inside containers molded to the precise measurements of their bodies, closing themselves inside, and remaining enclosed for thirty minutes. This first challenge is not as easy as it sounds for everyone; one of the contestants is claustrophobic, having entered the competition in an attempt to overcome his fear. During the "Box Challenge," the claustrophobic contestant stays in his container for only a few moments before a panic attack forces him to exit and receive medical attention. As he is the only contestant who does not complete this first "Box Challenge," the pilot episode ends with the other competitors voting the claustrophobic contestant *Outside the Box.*

Manhood 5

A sitcom in which a man tries to assert his masculinity in a culture that he views as increasingly unmasculine. In the pilot episode, The Masculine Man argues with his wife because she wants to paint their master bathroom pink. The Masculine Man says, "Pink is for women!" The Wife replies, "I am a woman." To which The Masculine Man says, "But I am a man and I forbid you to paint our bathroom pink." The Wife paints the bathroom pink, anyway, and when The Masculine Man uses the bathroom to defecate, The Audience howls with laughter because he is a masculine man, grunting and straining in a pink room. In later episodes, The Masculine Man will accuse his wife of trying to cut his penis off while he is sleeping (she was just trimming her toe nails), get in a fist fight with his neighbor during an argument about women and gays in the military, and lock his wife in a closet when he sees her smile during a conversation with another man. The Audience laughs and cheers as The Masculine Man endearingly asserts his manhood each week because they, too, men and women alike, believe that masculinity is under attack in America, and that steps need to be taken to make sure that men are allowed to be men. Each episode ends with The Wife serving The Masculine Man a rare steak, which he eats with his hands during the closing credits.

Clanking Replicator 6

In this quirky sitcom, ED-209 is a lonely robot living in a society of fruitful self-replicating robots. While the robots around him—namely ED-208 and ED-210—have self-replicated entire units of fellow robots with which to work and live, ED-209 has been unable to replicate a single companion. The series follows ED-209 as he works at a factory making replacement parts for robotic pets, spends time with his support group for non-replicating, self-replicating robots, and seeks companionship among his neighbors. In the pilot episode, ED-209 spends an afternoon with ED-208 and some of its replicated offspring—ED-208a, ED-208d, and ED-208i. When ED-209 makes a tasteless joke about RepRaps and their nonautonomous self-replication, ED-208 chastises ED-209 for obscuring his own insecurities by belittling others. ED-208 says, "01010011 01100101 01101100 01100110 00101101 01110010 01100101 01110000 01101100 01101001 01100011 01100001 01110100 01101001 01101111 01101110 00100000 01101001 01110011 00100000 01100001 00100000 01100110 01110101 01101110 01100100 01100001 01101101 01100101 01101110 01110100 01100001 01101100 00100000 01101110 01100101 01100011 01100101 01110011 01110011 01101001 01110100 01111001 00100000 01101111 01100110 00100000 01101111 01110101 01110010 00100000 01110011 01101111 01100011 01101001 01100101 01110100 01111001 00101100 00100000 01100001 01110101 01110100 01101111 01101110 01101111 01101101 01101111 01110101 01110011 00100000 01101111 01110010 00100000 01101110 01101111 01110100 00001010." The robot's words are subtitled on the bottom of the screen as, "Self-replication is a fundamental necessity of our society, autonomous or not." ED-208d adds, spoken in binary but subtitled as always,

"Those who cannot self-replicate endanger our culture." When ED-209 protests, ED-208i says, "When ED-208 ceases to function, we, his replications, will go on. When we cease to function, the replications we make will go on." Upset by its encounter with ED-208 et al, ED-209 visits ED-210 and asks for help learning how to self-replicate. Under the guidance of ED-210, ED-209 makes several attempts at self-replication. These attempts include building a robot with its outsides on its inside and its insides on its outside, building a robot with a cinder block where its head should be, building a robot with component parts made of brittle glass, and building a robot by fusing a central intelligence data processor to a living bird. These attempts are largely unsuccessful, though the robot-bird hybrid displays a brief flicker of artificial life, which causes ED-209 to feel a glimmer of hope that it will someday be able to participate in the self-replication upon which the continuation of robotic society relies.

Old Folks 7

A sitcom in which Ross and Jane, a couple in their seventies, come to terms with late-in-life independence after their children and grand-children stop visiting them. The pilot episode opens with Ross calling his adult children and inviting them over for dinner. Each invitation is met with a negative response, ranging from a simple, "No thanks," to the more colorful, "You know we can't visit because your age is a constant reminder of mortality, and every time we leave your house, our children can't sleep because they are afraid of death." After their invitations are refused, Ross and Jane decide to go out for a night on the town to try to recapture something of their youth. Unfortunately, they find that the restaurants and clubs they used to frequent have long closed. After a montage of jokes about Ross's bad driving and the couple's attempt to find an early bird dinner, Ross and Jane decide to visit a new bar called Vue. After waiting thirty minutes for a server, Ross goes to the bar to order drinks, but it is too dark and loud for him to read the price list, and he orders drinks that far exceed the amount of money he has in his wallet. Without credit cards, Ross is unable to pay for the drinks. Embarrassed by the situation, Ross retrieves Jane from their table, and the couple return home where they talk about friends and favorite stars who have died. Ross proposes that he and Jane are useless, and that maybe all the couple has left is to wait for death. Jane disagrees and suggests that, just because so many of their friends and favorite stars are dead, and just because their family and the world have left them behind, does not mean they are obsolete. The episode ends with Ross and Jane saying goodnight to pictures of their children and grandchildren hanging on their bedroom walls, then kissing each other on their mouths, and settling into sleep in their individual beds, just a few feet apart from each other in their master bedroom.

Men on the Moon 8

A speculative drama about the need for and build-up to the faked 1969 moon landing, and the subsequent fallout as experienced by the various conspirators involved with the forgery. The show works from the assumption—widely agreed upon, now—that the '69 moon landing was, indeed, faked, and explores why it was necessary for the United State government to create the illusion that American astronauts landed on the moon. After the fake landing is dramatized onscreen—this will happen around the time of the show's first season finale—the conspirators struggle to conceal the lie from their families and friends, as well as curious parties in the national media and dangerous foreign spies determined to ruin the United States' international reputation. The pilot episode begins with an urgent meeting, during which the president, vice president, and an assortment of government and military leaders discuss the failure of the United States' space program, the successes of the Soviet program, and the need for the U.S. to strike a decisive, symbolic blow against their enemies. This first scene ends with a cut to a Hollywood soundstage where a young art director is preparing a set of an alien planet for filming, while his friend, a special effects supervisor, prepares a model for an effects shot of a rocket landing. The men are approached by military officials and pulled into a conspiracy that will define a generation and change the course of history forever.

Mom vs. Dad 9

A family sitcom in which a mother and father attempt to settle their domestic arguments by attempting to kill one another. In the pilot episode, The Mother wants to enroll the youngest child—and only daughter—in dance classes. The Father believes The Daughter would be better suited to sports—softball, perhaps, or basketball, or maybe tennis. During the argument, The Mother tells The Father that he is a complete and utter failure at all things, and The Father tells The Mother that she is a bad mother and that he wishes she would die of pneumonia. The Mother responds by telling The Father that he might as well be dead with how useless he is. Following the fight, The Mother enlists the help of her daughter to kill The Father by covering his face with a pillow in his sleep. The Daughter is not strong enough and fails. The Father retaliates by asking his two sons to run a hose from the exhaust pipe of the family car up to the master bedroom while The Mother takes a nap. The Mother isn't really napping, though: She is hiding from her family, and is thus able to avoid dying from carbon monoxide poisoning. After this failure, the show segues into a montage during which beverages are poisoned; piranhas are released in a bathtub (they die); a sofa is filled with poisonous spiders; an explosive device is placed inside a pillow; and a trapdoor, leading to a vat of scalding hot water, is placed in the kitchen floor. By the end of the episode, both The Mother and The Father are sharing a hospital room—he covered in burns, she with a mild concussion and hearing loss from the weak explosive device that had been in her pillow. The Mother and The Father reconcile their differences and decide to ask The Daughter in which activity she wishes to participate. The Daughter wants to dance, and play lacrosse. At the beginning of the second episode, the physical damage The Mother and The Father inflicted on each other will be healed, and the process of mutual destruction will begin again.

I Love Lucy 10

This is neither a re-boot of the classic sitcom, nor a reimagining. The show is neither an adaptation, nor a remake. The new *I Love Lucy* will be a shot-for-shot re-presentation of the original series, in its entirety. The show's executive producer, Alain Menard, will arrive at the plot, shot composition, and editing of each episode from *I Love Lucy's* original run through a purely contemporary context. This new presentation of *I Love Lucy* will function as a scathing critique of fifties culture and nostalgia. Ricky's patriarchal attitudes will no longer be accepted as a manifestation of the era's sexual politics, but will be read as a critique of the era's misogyny. In this version of the show, the Ricardos' and Murtzs' trip to

Hollywood won't simply fetishize celebrity culture or function as a crass ratings grab, it will also function as a parody of historical attitudes toward fame, fortune, and the American dream. Iconic scenes from the original run of *I Love Lucy,* such as Lucy's first day on the job at the chocolate factory, and Lucy getting drunk while promoting Vitametavegamin in a television commercial, will be painstakingly imagined, filmed, and arrived at via Menard's contemporary vision of the Lucy character. In Menard's version, these scenes will be more than uproariously funny exercises in slapstick comedy—they will be read through lenses of late capitalism and substance abuse, respectively. It should be noted that the pilot episode of this show will not be seen until almost forty years after it is filmed, long after this new version of *I Love Lucy* finishes its run. The episode will be found under the bed of an actor who played a clown in the episode, to whom the only existing print of the episode will be given by the show's male and female leads. When the episode is found and airs, forty years from now, it will begin with this voiceover, the beginning of which will be lost due to the effects of time: "...Um, well she's... her hair is very red. And she's married to Ricky. In this district close to theaters and nightclubs where Ricky works, they have a little apartment where they laugh, love, and thoroughly enjoy life. They live in this apartment, here on the seventh floor. Now, let's look in on them." During the voiceover, we see various shots of a city's skyline before arriving at the described apartment. When the narrator suggests we "look in on the couple," a hand appears in front of the apartment and removes a wall. The first wall that The Hand removes is not the right wall, however, but after the narrator corrects The Hand, it removes the appropriate wall and the camera zooms in to find Lucy and Ricky getting out of their separate beds. The episode's plot revolves around Lucy trying to finagle a part in Ricky's nightclub act by impersonating the clown under whose bed the episode will be found many years later. Though this pilot episode will not air for forty years, the same story will be used and aired as the sixth episode in the show's first season.

Warp 11

An exploration-based science fiction show
that finds a spacecraft and crew making their
way through the universe and interfering
with other cultures. In the pilot episode, The
Liberty—the flagship of the United States of
America's Department of Space Exploration—
captained by former athlete and politician
Roger Jones, arrives at a planet known as L374,
which orbits Alpha Draconis, and is inhabited
by a species of reptilian humanoids known as
Draconians. The Draconians are believed to
have a secret presence on Earth because it is
their mission to undermine Earth's global
politics. Upon their arrival, Jones and his crew
discover that the Draconians are faced with
internal political troubles of their own. L374's

two primary political parties, the Librocrats— who believe in total liberty and personal responsibility, and the Progrocrats—who believe in a government-run society in which the weakest members of said society are cared for at the same level as the most powerful, are locked in a violent and dangerous power struggle, which is further exacerbated by the terrorist activities of a number of religiously minded extremist groups who believe that both the Librocrats and the Progrocrats have abandoned the culture's spiritual tenants in favor of secular concerns. Under the guise of diplomacy, Roger Jones offers to mediate a series of conversations between leaders from both political groups, while his crew supplies the religious extremists with weapons in an attempt to further destabilize the planet's troubled balance of power. Jones believes that upsetting the planet's political climate will subsequently hinder the Draconian's covert operations on Earth. Unfortunately for Jones and his crew, by strengthening the religious extremists' hand with Earth weapons and supplies, the Librocrats and Progrocrats are forced to put aside their differences and unite to defeat the dissidents. In the process, they discover that Earth has been supplying the terrorists, which leads to Alpha Draconis formally declaring war against Earth. The declaration of war establishes a seasonal arc that will build to an exciting two-hour finale.

Class Warfare 12

A reality-style game show of upward mobility in which contestants attempt to steal the fortunes of their bosses and other wealthy opponents through challenging them to feats of strength and contests of skill. Each episode is comprised of three challenges: one feat of strength designed by the challenger, and two contests of skill devised by the contestant who has been charged with defending his or her wealth. If the challenger wins two of the three contests, he or she acquires forty percent of the defender's net wealth. If the challenger loses, he or she is forced to act as the defender's personal servant for one year. In the first episode, a mail clerk, making seven-fifty an hour at a major corporation, challenges his

CEO to *Class Warfare*. For the feat of strength, the clerk challenges his boss to see who can carry the most gold bars twenty yards in sixty seconds. For his contests of skill, the CEO challenges the mail clerk to a doorman tipping contest, and a blind taste test of different caviar brands. During the feat of strength, the mail clerk's chances of untold wealth and power are jeopardized when he learns that gold bars weigh far more than the packages he delivers for his job. The clerk's bid for wealth seems to be further imperiled when he is unable to eat his caviar samples, finding both the taste and texture unpleasant. The Audience will learn during a cut-away, however, that the clerk's inability to eat the caviar makes no difference as, having never before eaten caviar, he would have been guessing anyway. After two difficult challenges, the clerk, who is friendly and charming, excels at tipping the doorman. At the conclusion of the three challenges, the show's host reveals the final scores of each contest, and a winner is named.

Nuts & Bolts 13

In this sci-fi drama with comedic undertones, a family of androids attempts to fit into a small, Midwestern suburb. Due to anti-android sentiment, the family of four—a mother, father, son, and daughter—attempts to conceal their true nature from those around them. In the pilot episode, the family's secret is jeopardized when The Son goes out for his high school's baseball team and, despite his slight physique and reputation as a bookworm, outperforms even the school's best athletes. After intense scrutiny and the threat of a physical and drug test—both circumvented by The Son's decision to remove himself from consideration for the team—The Son and The Mother share a heartwarming conversation about their need to avoid scrutiny by keeping a certain distance from the town's other residents, and maintaining the appearance of their own mediocrity. "We know how strong we are," The Mother says. "And as long as we remember that, it doesn't matter how we look to humans." Of course, the family's secret will be constantly endangered by a nosy, suspicious neighbor's comedic attempts to unearth the android family's true nature. As the series progresses, the desires of The Father and his children to overcome their alienation will lead to a variety of dramatic and comedic situations—The Father participates in a hot dog-eating contest, The Son courts a human girlfriend, The Daughter joins the school's chess club—through which the android family's humanity is tested. The series asks the question: is it possible that these androids, trying to appear human, are more human than the flesh and blood humans surrounding them? Human?

Sober 14

A sitcom about a relationship between an effeminate man and his recovering alcoholic girlfriend who is prone to relapses. The couple, who have lived together for several years before the series begins, share a deep-seated contempt for each other. Each episode is about the couple's failure to trust each other. In the pilot episode, the boyfriend brings home flowers to spruce up the couple's drab apartment only to find that The Recovering Alcoholic Girlfriend Who Is Prone to Relapses Is passed out drunk on the kitchen floor. When The Recovering Alcoholic Girlfriend Who Is Prone to Relapses wakes up, she calls her boyfriend a pussy for buying flowers, which the audience finds quite funny. Then she eats an entire box of Triscuits—which the audience finds even funnier because recovering alcoholics who have relapses are funny when they eat triscuits—and goes to the toilet to be sick. The boyfriend holds The Recovering Alcoholic Girlfriend Who Is Prone to Relapses's hair back while she is sick. The audience laughs because the effeminate boyfriend looks away and holds his nose while The Recovering Alcoholic Girlfriend Who Is Prone to Relapses vomits. Later, the couple reaches an agreement in which the boyfriend will try harder to be a good partner, and The Recovering Alcoholic Girlfriend Who Is Prone to Relapses will only relapse during Network Sweeps months. Future episodes revolve around a variety of amusing situations, such as the couple's bitter argument after being refused the right to adopt a son, the boyfriend's struggles to fit in with The Recovering Alcoholic Girlfriend Who Is Prone to Relapses's cocaine-addled friends, and a trip to a baseball game at which The Recovering Alcoholic Girlfriend Who Is

Prone to Relapses relapses by drinking the remnants of beer cups left around the couple's seats. The baseball episode features a guest appearance by The Famous Baseball Player Who Is Also a Recovering Addict, who speaks out against the dangers of substance abuse.

Credit Busters 15

A reality-style game show in which two challengers, competing head-to-head, attempt to accrue as much debt as possible by purchasing an assortment of high-end consumer goods. The winning debtor receives debt consolidation services and all interest paid on his or her purchases until said purchases are paid off, while the loser is left to be crushed beneath the weight of so much debt. The first segment of each episode follows contestants as they attempt to acquire enough credit—both through establishing multiple lines, and receiving high limits on those lines—to effectively accrue the debt needed to win. In each episode's second segment, the contestants spend money on various luxury goods, the camera lingering, lovingly, on each item. Finally, every episode ends with a tally of how much the contestants spent, and a declaration of the winner. In the pilot episode, the winning contestant works with five different credit cards and two loans to purchase a 46" Yalos Diamond flat-screen television (studded with 160 twenty-karat diamonds); a Beefeater Gold Plated Barbecue Grill; a pair of dress shoes by Testoni; one semester of coursework at Fordham University; season tickets, behind home plate, for the New York Yankees; and a house. The loser of the contest attempts to outspend his rival by sending elaborate floral arrangements to every person he has ever met, and purchasing 500,000 butterflies to release throughout the New York City subway system during peak hours. Unfortunately, the second contestant loses and learns that it may have been a better strategy to purchase goods that could be returned instead of the pure but fleeting manifestations of beauty on which he spent his money. The winning contestant returns and cancels many of his purchases at the end of the episode, but retains his Yankees tickets and his Testoni dress shoes. The losing contestant, having made the world a more beautiful place for as many people as he could, takes his own life after realizing he is millions of dollars in debt.

Edward and Regina 16

A sitcom in which a married couple love and respect each other, and are trying to start a family. In the pilot episode, Edward and Regina return home from work around the same time and calmly discuss the logistics of having a baby. Edward believes he is emotionally ready, but is worried that they are not yet financially stable enough to provide for a child. Regina agrees, but thinks the couple should begin building a nursery in their guestroom and saving money from their paychecks so they will be ready sooner rather than later. The episode culminates with the couple imagining the nursery, and then imagining the baby inside of it. Then the couple imagines the nursery without a baby. This is a sad and lonely thing to imagine. The couple decides it would be strange to build a nursery without a baby on the way, and they do not want to pressure themselves in this manner. Instead of building the nursery, Edward and Regina decide to play tennis together. After tennis, the couple returns home and has sex with each other, using contraception. Those who have seen advanced screeners of the pilot episode appreciate its strong craft and mature tone, but do not expect *Edward and Regina* to go into production.

Up in Arms 17

In this irreverent sitcom, a construction worker who has lost both of his arms in a freak accident attempts to sort through his anger, find a new place for himself, and maintain his independence in a world built by and for people with arms. The pilot episode opens with The Construction Worker opening mail with his feet. In one of the envelopes, he finds his first workers' compensation check. The Construction Worker gets down on his knees, picks the check up with his mouth and carries it to the bank. The Audience laughs when The Construction Worker attempts to endorse the check using a pen clenched between his teeth. He cannot sign his name; only scribble unintelligible lines. When The Construction

Worker approaches the counter, The Bank Teller, an attractive young woman, takes the check out of his mouth and asks if he would like to deposit it in checking or savings. "Checking," he says. "Can I help you with anything else?" The Bank Teller asks. Through a cut-away montage, we see The Construction Worker imagining The Bank Teller opening a door for him, retrieving objects off of shelves, washing his back in the shower, unzipping his pants so that he can go to the restroom, folding his laundry, changing the channel on his television, getting his wallet out of his back pocket, and holding an ice cream cone to his mouth so he can eat it. At the end of the montage, The Construction Worker says, "No, thank you." On his way home from the bank, The Construction Worker finds a turtle on the sidewalk. He wants to help the turtle to a pond or creek, but doesn't know how without arms. After several attempts to pick up the turtle with his feet and mouth—each met with uproarious laughter from The Audience—The Construction Worker finds a trash-can lid nearby. He guides the turtle into the lid and pushes the lid down the street with his feet. When he returns to his apartment building, he pushes the lid into the elevator then down the hall to his apartment. There, The Construction Worker lies on his back and uses his feet to unlock and open his door. He pushes the lid to his bathroom, draws a shallow bath—using the side of his face to start and stop the water—then lifts the turtle into the tub with his feet. The episode ends with The Construction Worker kissing the turtle on the head. The Audience says, "Awwwwwww."

Regrets 18

A reality show in which subjects close to death discuss their regrets and deliver farewell messages to their loved ones. In the pilot episode, a retired school teacher has learned that she has an inoperable brain tumor that will soon end her life. The woman tells the camera crew that she regrets not being a better mother; that she regrets not retiring earlier; that she regrets telling people that she prefers Colby to American cheese for most of her life because it was a lie meant to protect her from the embarrassment of loving a cheese meant for children; that she regrets uprooting a neighbor's rose bushes during a property line dispute in the seventies; that she regrets seeing some movies a second time in the theater because the second time was always the same as the first time; that she regrets not loving her husband better, but regrets not loving herself better more; that she regrets not staying in better touch with her children; that she regrets spending so many of her final days filming for a reality show that she will never see, that her children and grandchildren will probably never watch; that she regrets being so maudlin; that she regrets being so critical of herself; that she doesn't regret reading *The Crying of Lot 49* in college, but she regrets reading the ending because she liked believing that the novel would have a clearer resolution than it does; that she regrets not being born twenty years earlier or thirty years later; that she regrets that she regrets that she regrets...

Primetime 19

In this family sitcom, thirteen-year-old pop-culture obsessive Kyle attempts to navigate the ins and outs of living with his broken family. Kyle's mother and father are separated, and he and his older siblings (a fifteen-year-old brother and a seventeen-year-old sister) split their time between their parents' homes. Kyle's sister is indifferent to him, and his brother dislikes him, blaming him for the dissolution of their parents' marriage. For the parents' part, Kyle's mother is forgetful and uninterested in the pop culture with which Kyle is obsessed, and his father isn't interested in Kyle because his son doesn't enjoy sports. To make matters worse, Kyle's lack of interest in sports and video games makes him fairly unpopular at school, and he only has one friend, an overweight Harry Potter super-fan named Peter. Combining his fandom with his name, the kids at school refer to Peter as Harry Peter. The other kids at school are fully aware that the nickname refers to genetalia. Peter, however, likes the nickname because of his love of all things relating to Harry Potter. Even though he has Peter, Kyle still spends a great deal of time by himself and often spends his afternoons fantasizing that he is the main characters from some of his favorite television shows. In the pilot episode, Kyle and Peter get in a fight after Kyle tries to tell Peter what his nickname really means. When Kyle goes home to his mom's, she is busy playing solitaire and doesn't have time to talk with her son about his day. Kyle's sister isn't home either—she never is—and when Kyle tries to go to his bedroom, which he shares with his brother, said brother punches Kyle in the stomach and calls him a fag. With nowhere to go, Kyle spends the afternoon in the linen closet of his mother's apartment and delivers several of Cosmo Kramer's monologues from *Seinfeld*, then pretends to be a cylon from the original *Battlestar Galactica*, which he is not very good at because it hurts his voice to talk like they did. When Kyle feels like crying, he gives the eulogy from the funeral scene in the episode of *The Mary Tyler Moore Show* called "Chuckle Bites the Dust." In that episode, Mary Richards is trying to not laugh during Chuckles the Clown's funeral. When Mary Richards finally loses control and laughs, the priest says that Chuckles "found tears very offensive," that the clown "hated to see people cry." Then the priest tells Mary Richards to "go ahead, my dear, laugh for Chuckles," at which time all Mary Richards is able to do is cry, and cry, and cry. When Kyle reenacts this part of the episode he cries and cries and cries. This is where the pilot episode ends. Subsequent episodes follow in kind.

JAMES BRUBAKER lives in Oklahoma with his wife. His short stories have appeared or are forthcoming in venues including *Zoetrope: All Story*, *Michigan Quarterly Review*, *The Normal School*, *Hayden's Ferry Review*, *Indiana Review*, *Web Conjunctions*, *Sundog Lit*, *Keyhole*, and *The Texas Review*, among others. His short story collection, *Liner Notes*, will be published by Subito Press later in 2014.